Surfer Dog

ELIZABETH SPURR

SCHOLASTIC INC.

New York Toronto London Auckland Sydney
Mexico City New Delhi Hong Kong Buenos Aires

ISBN 0-439-40481-9

12 11 10 9 8 7 6 5 4 3 2   3 4 5 6 7 8/0

Printed in the U.S.A.   40

First Scholastic printing, March 2003
Designed by Richard Amari

Major props to Mattie, my surf-shredding son

Contents

Surfer Dog

1 A New Friend

No one believes me when I tell them. But so what? It's true. I'd swear it on my new tri-fin.

My dog, Blackie, knows how to surf.

Come on, Pete, they say, not another boring pet trick.

No way. My dog not only can time waves perfectly, he even taught *me*. I guess he taught me some other things, too. Which sort of changed my whole life. Which pretty much needed it.

It's a fantastic day for surfing—bright sun and glassy sea, with September's warm offshore breezes shaping the waves into perfect blue-green tubes. They say Whaler's Cove has the best surf on the Central Coast, but it's been flat or blown out since we moved here last month. Now, at last, a perfect Saturday. I can't wait to hit the beach.

I pedal along Ocean Avenue, park and lock my bike by

the pier. CREEASH! This huge wave shakes all the pilings, sprays all the fishermen. If only Skip were here, he'd lose it.

It was tough leaving my friends in L.A.; I've been pretty depressed. But I guess Dad's right. We're lucky to be able to move away from crowds and smog. Everything will be great, I keep telling myself, once I get to know a few people. But right now, after two weeks in school, I'm still the invisible man. I spend all lunch hour alone, walking around kind of fast, like I've got somewhere to go, someone to meet. I wonder if I'm fooling anyone.

Main Beach is pretty crowded, mostly with surfers who have a few years on me. I look over the guys in wet suits, looking for the hotshots I've read about in *Surfer*. I've heard they hang out here.

Sure enough, there's Mike Grimsby, can't miss the red hair. And the tall dark one—that has to be Jaime Lozano. No question, Main Beach is the spot!

After waxing my board, I wade in. The cold water's kind of a shock, has to be fifteen degrees cooler than in Southern California, and me with a leak in my wet suit.

I paddle out, catch a five-foot left-hander, do a couple of cutbacks, and am looking good. I'm on the lip and—oops—"Sorreee!" I run smack into a goofy-foot show-off, riding the right peak.

"Watch it, grommet!" he yells.

"Yeah, inlander," calls a big tan blond. "Move it down to the kiddie bowl."

The goofy-foot jerks his chin south; a couple of others point.

"Sure, okay," I say, pretty embarrassed. So much for surfing with the big guns.

About two hundred yards south of Main Beach jetty, the shore is gradual, the waves like ripples—a great place for beginners. But that's not me. I've surfed all the hot spots in Southern California: Huntington Beach, the Newport jetties, Trestles.

Skip's older brother, Hughie, took us surfing every weekend. They called Skip and me the Junior Geronimos. No one down south tried to shoo us off, not even at Black's or Swami's.

Surfers aren't really snobs; they just like to protect their territory. Skimming around with my ninety-three pounds, I look about eight instead of eleven. I hope these guys at Whaler's Cove can get beyond the puny build, notice my cutbacks and aerials. I don't want to come off like a wannabe pest.

Right now I'm ready to back off; no use getting pushy my first day out. I pick up my board and head south.

The beginners' beach is jammed, a dozen guys surfing out of control, boards flying. Belly boarders. Even girls on rubber mattresses. Like the bunny hill on the ski slope—pretty dangerous.

No way am I going to risk it. I turn back, pass Main Beach, and head toward the cove at Mouse Rock, north of the pier.

There the waves are breaking at three feet. The sea's as smooth as a bathtub. No riptides. A lot safer than surfing with beginners. Maybe just this once I'll forget my folks' no-no: Never surf alone.

But wait. There *is* someone. A dark head pops from the surf, about a hundred yards up the beach. A bodysurfer. A wave swoops him up, crests, and drops him into a mess of churning foam. He turns and goes for another.

Good ride. Good swimmer. Maybe the two of us can look after each other.

Just so the other guy stays out of my way.

For some reason, I'm on today. I'm catching every wave in sight, dropping in late, powering off the bottom, and smacking the lip. Long, smooth rides. I wish there were a tent of judges watching. Or the guys at Main Beach. The way I'm ripping today, they'd for sure change their minds.

I slide into shore, straddle my board between a rock and a log, and go for my water bottle. Then I put on more sunscreen. Being kind of pale, I freckle and peel like crazy.

My watch says only 10:30, but my stomach says noon. I'm always hungry and eat a ton, but I can't seem to put on weight. Mom says I could sell my secret for a million bucks.

I retrieve my lunch from a crack in the rock. Maybe just a half sandwich. And a pickle. And a cookie. I could marf the whole thing but get a grip on myself and put the sack back in its hiding place. I peel off the wet suit and lie on my towel. The salt drying on my back prickles my skin.

I hear footsteps, then some rustling. Someone kicks

sand on my legs. The whole beach, and that one guy has to trip over me.

I raise up on one elbow. "Hey, dude . . ."

Almost in my face is a large wet dog, a slick black Labrador with bulging brown eyes and a flapping tail.

"Well, hi, fella!"

The dog whimpers and licks my mouth.

"Hey, easy. I mean, I like you and all, but . . ."

The dog straightens and sniffs the air, tail still wagging big time. Then, nose up, he heads for the lunch bag in the crevice. He stands on his hind legs and paws the sack till it drops. Then, with his jaws clamped around it, he bounds down the beach.

"Hey, mutt. No fair!" I run after him, but the dog streaks like a racehorse. I give up and whistle through my teeth. "Here, Blackie. Come on, boy!"

And guess what? The dog skids to a stop, turns in his tracks, and trots back. He drops the lunch at my feet.

"Wow! Good boy, Blackie."

The dog pants and wags his tail and tries to shake hands.

"Is that your name? Blackie?"

The dog perks up his ears, then sits. He sniffs at the sack but doesn't touch it. With his tail brushing the sand, he looks up with hungry eyes.

"Okay, boy. I guess you deserve it." I reach into the bag and hold out the half sandwich, starting in on the second half myself. "Like tuna?"

Blackie wolfs down the sandwich in one bite.

After lunch I take my board and wade back into the water. The dog follows.

The waves have grown larger, and the other surfer isn't around. Maybe I'd better move closer to Main Beach. "Come on, boy." But Blackie doesn't follow. Instead, he swims through the surf and heads toward an oncoming swell.

I watch him paddle, then turn as the wave peaks. Pulled up to the crest, he plunges back toward the shore. His timing is perfect.

He struggles through the surf and dashes over, showering me as his lean body shakes off the drops.

"Hey, good ride, dude!"

The dog gives his paw for a shake, then turns toward the waves again.

"No, boy. Let's go."

Blackie is already swimming toward the rock. I watch him bob through the swells, and finally it dawns on me. That dark-headed surfer must have been the dog.

After one more ride, and a couple of loud whistles, Blackie follows me to Main Beach. He doesn't have a collar, so I wade past the guys, calling, "Anyone own this dog?" That's one way to get acquainted.

Some of them stop to pet Blackie. "Hey, great pooch." But no one's seen him before.

The tide turns, and the waves begin pumping. Blackie gets impatient with wading. He barks at me, then plunges into the surf, about thirty feet south of the surfers.

I follow him, paddling way beyond the breakline. The

dog swims in circles while I straddle the board. Then all of a sudden he whimpers and noses seaward. Sure enough, a big old set of swells is moving in.

Blackie drifts over the first and second swell, then paddles like fury toward shore. I do the same. We both catch wave number three right on the peak and sail into shore past a whole line of boards.

I see my chance to do a little fancy work. I throw a couple of quick slashes and end with a frontside aerial, which I stick.

When I finally sink into a foot of water, one of the guys puts up a thumb and calls, "Grr-eat ride!" But I see he's looking at the dog.

Blackie and I move down the beach, out of the way of the hotshots. The waves aren't quite as hollow, but I can't risk getting in the way.

The dog never seems to tire. I surf a full hour more, with him close beside me, except a couple of times when Blackie catches the wave I've missed.

He paddles round and round between sets, his eyes always returning seaward. It must be hard to keep going with no board to rest on. He could use a life-preserver jacket. If he were mine, I'd buy him one. *If* he were mine.

Pretty soon Blackie's getting lots of attention. "Hey, that's quite the pup!" I can feel the surfers watching as, over and over, Blackie follows me into shore, like I'm his master.

Blackie's master. That's what I am. At least till Mom has her say.

2 Finders Keepers?

Mom's getting ready for a dinner party. Her hair smells like the beauty salon, and she's in her cooking sweat suit, the sleeves covered with red spots that match the sauce on the stove. She's setting the table with her new pottery and place mats. I can smell a pie in the oven.

I'd hosed the sand off myself and the dog, then shut Blackie in the laundry room.

"Don't track up my floor," says Mom, her usual greeting.

"I dried off," I say, still toweling my wet suit. "I have something to show you."

"Later, okay?" Mom opens the oven and sticks a toothpick into the pecan pie.

"But Mom, it's important."

"Later!"

A thump comes from the laundry room.

"What's that?"

"Come see."

I open the door. Blackie waggles into the kitchen, skidding on the newly waxed floor. He noses Mom's crotch.

"Pete! Where in the . . . ?"

"Found him at the beach."

"How dare you bring a smelly, wet dog into my kitchen?"

"He doesn't smell."

"Take him out! Now!"

I give a low whistle. "Come, Blackie."

The dog obeys just like that. I shut the laundry room door. "See what a good dog he is?"

"All the way out," says Mom. "To the yard."

I take Blackie outside. When I get back, Mom's taking the pie from the oven. She looks like she's going to cry. "Now look what you've done. I almost burned it."

"I like 'em crispy."

Mom turns and put her hands on my shoulders, like she's going to shake me. But she doesn't. "I'll crisp *you*, Peter Fox!"

"Hey, Mom?" No question, she's weirded out today.

Mom sighs, put her arms around the wet suit. "Sorry," she breathes. "Guess I'm nervous about tonight. I don't know these people very well." She tastes a crumb from the crust. "Making new friends isn't all that easy."

"You got that right." If she thinks the Yacht Club's tough, she ought to try Seaview School.

"You *have* that right," Mom corrects. She used to teach third grade and is a stickler for grammar. "Well, at least

I'm making an effort." Meaning, why don't I go out for team sports.

At first I did make an effort. I hung around the soccer field every noon. But when the guys chose up sides, it was like I wasn't there. When all the spots were filled, they'd say, "Sorry, next time!" Finally, one day they had a spot, but I saw the guys drawing straws for whose team would take the runt. I went to the can and never came back.

Mom puts the pie on the counter to cool. Right off, a large black head and two paws appear at the windowsill. Mom smiles, but just barely. "Good sniffer, I see."

I move the pie; Blackie's eyes follow it. "He's a great dog."

"Looks like a purebred," says Mom. "You'd better call the Humane Society right away. Someone's probably frantic."

"I'm starving. What's to eat?"

"I mean now." She hands me the phone.

"Where's the phone book?"

"Right where it always is."

I look up the number and glance at the clock. In ten minutes the Humane Society will be closed. I head for the refrigerator.

"Now!" says Mom.

While she decorates her pâté with parsley, I dial and get a recording and a bunch of numbers to press, which I do, but my hand's shaking. Finally a human woman answers.

"We want to report a lost dog. . . . A black Labrador. Male. . . . No collar." After I answer all the questions, I put down the phone and try not to smile. "They can't pick him up till Monday."

Mom looks at the dog, who's wagging his tail and looking at Mom with his bulgy brown eyes. She melts a little. "Guess we'd better buy a small bag of kibble."

"They say to keep him confined."

She sighs and wipes her forehead with her sleeve. "Take the old blue blanket from the linen closet. You can make him a bed in the garage."

I make my dog a nice bed in the garage from a down quilt covered with the old blue blanket. After Blackie circles and snuggles down, I ride my bike to the market for kibble. And a can of Gourmet Dog Feast. And a package of liver-flavored dog treats. Blackie's all mine, at least till Monday. And I'll have a whole day tomorrow to show my folks how special he is.

If the party goes well, Mom will be in a good mood. Maybe she'll let me keep Blackie, at least till his owner is found. Then I'll cross my fingers and toes and eyeballs that no owner shows up.

Some chance. More like a miracle. This dog is a real winner: beautiful, smart, well trained. And a great surfer, to boot. Someone, somewhere has to be missing him something awful.

"We should put up signs downtown," says Mom. "You can make them on your computer, Pete. 'FOUND: Black Labrador.'"

I pick a couple of raisins from my bran muffin.

"'Found Dog' might be better," says Dad. "Lots of people want black Labradors."

"I'll do it this afternoon," I say. "Right now the surf's pumping."

"It won't take that long," says Mom, who's on to me. "Dad and I can post them."

Mom pours Dad a second cup of coffee. "I'll call the *Tribune* tomorrow. They run 'Found' ads for free."

Dad stirs his coffee even though he takes it black. "What time is the Humane Society coming tomorrow?"

"But, dear," says Mom, "what if no one adopts him?" Mom looks out to the yard, where Blackie is attacking an old tennis ball. "These days they only keep dogs for two weeks. And then . . . well, you know."

I cringe but keep quiet.

Dad tastes his coffee. Still too hot; it fogs his glasses. "Good dog like that, there won't be a problem."

The tennis ball conquered, Blackie looks toward the kitchen, spots Mom, wags his tail. "He *is* a lovely dog, isn't he? No reason we can't keep him till the owner calls."

I take heart. Mom's party must have been a success.

Upstairs I run off a few Found Dog signs, then change into my wet suit; I can't wait to surf with Blackie again.

The lady at the Humane Society said to keep him confined. But I know Blackie. He won't leave me; he's *my* dog now.

Almost.

3 Whose Dog?

Look, Pete, look what I found!" Mom hustles into the kitchen, loaded with packages. Blackie, dragging his new leash, follows her.

She opens one of the plastic bags. "A battery-heated blanket. Winter's coming. It'll keep him warm and cozy."

"Yeah."

"Don't you like it?"

I can't get all excited. For the last few weeks Mom's been haunting the pet store. Blackie now has a wicker dog bed with BLACKIE stitched on the mattress. A studded leather collar with a heart-shaped tag. And his own toy box filled with stuff like squeaky cats that he can demolish with a couple of good chomps.

During the past few weeks we've had a lot of calls for a Found Dog, but only one for a Labrador, a golden female. I can't believe our luck.

Every day we discover new Blackie tricks. He can let

himself in and out by turning the door handle with his teeth. He fetches the morning paper without being told. And for a dog biscuit he'll spin in midair like a dancer. Otherwise, he never begs for food; instead, he lies quietly under the dinner table. What a champ. I'm pretty nuts about him. But so is Mom. That's my problem.

She babies Blackie to death, cooks him beef hearts and chicken giblets, says they "prevent fleas." She's put a snapshot of the dog in her wallet, next to mine. She's even bought one of those dumb bumper stickers, I ♡ LABS.

"You should see what Blackie did today, Pete." Mom's unloading cans and cartons into the pantry cupboard, her healthy diet food on the left, good stuff to the right. "I was about to cross Sixth and Ocean, when he comes to a dead stop. Sits on the curb and won't budge. Just then a car roars around the corner doing about fifty. We might have been hit."

"Good dog," I say, only half listening.

"You betcha, good doggums." She blows a few kisses his way.

"Mom," I say. "When's it going to be *my* turn?"

Mom just looks at me, her blue eyes round and blank like in cartoons.

"Every day you take Blackie off to the bank, the post office, the cleaners."

"The whole town loves him," she says. "He sits so nicely outside the stores. Never moves a paw."

"Can I take him surfing tomorrow afternoon?"

"As if you had to ask."

She brings Blackie's bowl from the laundry room and fills it with vitamin-enriched kibble. "But I *had* hoped to take him to Jazzercize. The girls all love Blackie." My mother calls all the women "girls," even the wrinkled, fat ones.

Mom doesn't understand. I *need* to take Blackie surfing. When he's around, the guys even talk to me. Not much, but at least I'm not ignored, like at school. But I don't dare complain about Seaview. I don't need another lecture about team sports.

"Mom, *whose* dog is he?"

"He's *our* dog."

"*I* found him."

She makes Blackie sit and speak, then puts down his bowl. "*I'm* the one who takes care of him."

"You won't let me."

"You can't cook," she says.

"I could give him baths."

"The groomer says he needs oil treatments. The salt water dries his skin." She scratches Blackie behind the ears. He licks her hand. "I don't think you should take him swimming so often."

"Mom! He's a surfer dog. That's his life!"

"That's *your* life, Pete. As for Blackie, I think he enjoys Jazzercize just as much. Did I tell you, he thumps his tail to the music?"

After dinner I haul the doggie bed and the battery

blanket to my room. After hassling for more than an hour, Mom and I have worked out a truce. I write it down so she can't get on my case.

THE DOG-MA CARTA

1. During the school year Mom may cart the dog anywhere she wants weekdays between the hours 8:00 A.M. and 3:00 P.M.

2. After 3:00 P.M. weekdays and all day on weekends, Pete has full possession of Blackie.

3. After 6:00 P.M. on weekdays, Blackie becomes property of Mom and Dad until all homework is completed.

4. Blackie may stay in Pete's room at night, but must sleep on his own mattress.

I run a copy of the Dog-Ma Carta from my printer and tack it on my bulletin board.

Dad sticks his head in the door. "Good night, son." He sees the dog, lying on his mattress in the corner. "What's going on?"

"Our new Dog-Ma Carta." I hand him a copy.

He looks it over and laughs, although I know he can't read without his glasses. "Glad you're keeping your mother in line."

After Mom has looked in, I pull the covers from the foot of the bed. I take the doggie mattress from the corner and lay it next to the footboard. I motion to Blackie, "Come, boy."

He hesitates, too well trained to jump on the bed. "Come on, boy, it's okay."

When Blackie is settled on his mattress, I tuck the covers over him and slide into bed.

Mom can have no beef. I've obeyed Rule No. 4.

That night I dream Blackie and I are surfing Main Beach with Grimsby and Lozano and the goofy foot. I'm ripping big time and getting major props until a twenty-footer grinds me into the sand. My board's on top of me; I can't move, and here comes another wave to pound me. I yell for help, but the guys pretend not to hear me; they pack up their boards and leave.

I wake up on the floor, my heart playing bongo drums, Blackie licking my face. And I wonder, if I got into trouble, is that the way it would play? Maybe they'd all laugh when the goofy foot says, "Smart-ass kid, it serves him right."

And there I am, with only Blackie to care.

4 Blackie to the Rescue

Sunday afternoon we find super-low minus tides. Blackie and I wade through the tide pools that surround Mouse Rock, where the water is usually eight to ten feet deep. The sky is bright blue, the air still and smelling of seaweed. There are lots of families poking around, parents showing little kids the anemones, starfish, and mussels that cling to the volcanic formations along the shore.

I've brought sandwiches for me and Blackie, my Walkman radio, and a paperback copy of *Robinson Crusoe.* It's my favorite. I've read it three times, but my book report's a week overdue. Why can't we just read books for fun? Instead, we have to pick each one apart till it turns boring.

Blackie and I climb about forty feet to a flat spot near the top of Mouse Rock, between the ears of the mouse's head. The day is so clear I can see all the way to Crystal Bay.

Mouse Rock is about a block north of Main Beach, where I left my board. Most of the surfers are taking a lunch break, waiting for the tide to turn and bring larger waves. So far the sets have been nowhere, the water calm as a lake. The predicted south swell, caused by a storm off Baja California, has failed to show up.

I'm still surfing pretty much on my own, keeping out of the hotshots' way, waiting for some great waves, hoping to show them what I can do. Today's swell might be my chance—if it doesn't pass us by.

I strip off my wet-suit top, polish off my lunch, and stretch out on my towel with *Robinson Crusoe*. Each time I think about life on a desert island, I see Blackie as my man Friday. After three chapters the warm sun puts me to sleep, with Blackie dozing on a ledge several feet below.

Splash! A rain of ocean spray wakes me. The tide has come in, the waves are crashing below, churning just beneath the ledge where Blackie was resting. He's no longer there.

"Blackie!" I whistle through my fingers. "Blackie!" From the beach comes a loud bark. My dog is pacing the wet sand, about fifty feet from the rock, dodging the waves as they tear at the shore.

Smart dog. Smarter than his master. But what do I do now?

I zip into my wet suit, tucking the book and Walkman against my chest, then tie the towel around my waist.

No question, the south swell is here. Waves of eight to ten feet smash against the rock, with a force that would bruise and bloody any swimmer. Blackie escaped just in time.

Now the rock is completely surrounded by churning water, the sand a good fifty feet away. The rock on the lee side, toward the beach, is too steep to climb down; in fact, it's inverted. And the water is too shallow to jump into from that height.

On the seaward side, I try creeping down toward the boiling mass of foam. Could I swim in between waves? Maybe. But I'd have to dive into water that might be hiding a reef. And if I try to edge down slowly, a wave might pound me into the rocks.

A wall of water looms. I scramble to the top of the rock and cling to one of the mouse ears. The water beats against the ledge behind me, spraying foam high into the air. Heavy drops rain down on me; salt water stings my eyes. If the tide rises higher, if the waves get stronger, I could easily be washed from my perch.

"Blackie, help!"

He barks at me and bounds in a circle.

I can see the surfers along the shoreline beyond the pier. I wave both arms like a wild man, "Help!" but the booming surf drowns my shouts.

Blackie lets out a long howl, then charges at full speed to Main Beach. I cling to the rock like a barnacle and watch my dog. With yelps and nudges, he's getting the surfers' attention!

The next thing I know, three of them are running toward Mike Grimsby's Jeep. Grimsby, I've heard, works as lifeguard here every summer. He grabs the wheel and speeds the Jeep down the beach.

Two of the surfers inflate a rubber lifeboat. Grimsby throws me a coil of heavy rope and calls, "Tie it around one of the mouse ears!"

Between waves, Grimsby paddles the boat and anchors it on the lee side of the rock. He holds the rope and shouts, "Shimmy on down."

I look down at the bouncing boat, a good thirty-five feet below. Another wave dashes against the rock. I can't stop shaking.

Sure, just slide down. What if the knot comes loose? Or the rope frays? What if I can't hang on? I picture falling into the shallow water that covers the sharp rocks. I see my bloody body piled into an ambulance. I see a hospital, a funeral parlor, a casket.

"No fear, dude," calls Grimsby. "You can do it!"

Blackie runs in circles on the beach, barking, like he's cheering me on. I can do it. I have to do it. Like I have a choice?

I take a deep breath, sit down on the rock, and grip the rope. I keep my eyes on the rock, not daring to look below. I slide, five, ten, fifteen feet. "Owww!" The rope burns my hands. I stop, dangling above Grimsby's head. My fingers are on fire.

"Good going. You're almost here."

I shut my eyes and loosen my grip. The next thing I know, I've fallen on top of Grimsby, knocked him over, and capsized the boat.

The water churns around us, bouncing the boat out of reach and knocking us into the rocks. We struggle to keep afloat until the water quiets and ebbs, then swim as fast as we can to the shore, pulling ourselves out just as the next big one hits. Pow! The boat flies into the air, skids off a jagged reef, is swallowed by wild waves. Grimsby shrugs. "Could have been us, pal!"

One of the surfers, who's a stringer for the newspaper, snaps a few shots of Grimsby, Blackie, and me. "See ya in the funnies," he calls, and heads for his car.

Uh-oh. Wait till Mom and Dad see the story. Nothing funny about that.

The boat is finally tossed ashore by the raging surf. I watch Grimsby as he deflates it and finishes his rescue report. He's short, with a strong, stocky build and a sunburn as red as his hair. He always looks like he's smiling, even when he's not. Right now he grins at the report, then lays the clipboard on the deck of the lifeguard shelter, next to Blackie.

"That's some dog."

"Yeah." I stare out to sea, not wanting to face the guy. The waves are peaking at around ten feet, and here Grimsby has to spend time rescuing a scared kid, a doofus who can't even slide down a rope.

"I keep thinking," says Grimsby, "that I've seen Blackie somewhere before."

My heart does a double cutback. "Yeah?"

"But then," he adds, "all black Labs look alike."

Another gigantic wave pounds the shore, thrashing several surfers in its wake and giving the hotshots a twelve-foot drop. One disappears into a gaping backdoor barrel.

I stand up, feeling a little rubber-legged. "Guess we'd better get on home. Give you a chance to catch some big ones."

"Hey, the swell's just beginning. Why don't we take a few?"

We? Grimsby wants to surf with *me*?

"Well . . ." Am I up to the big swell? Haven't I disgraced myself enough for one day?

"Come on, Pete. I've been watching. You and Blackie can handle them."

Grimsby is actually asking the doofus to ride these wild storm waves. The doofus and Blackie, that is.

I swallow the frog in my voice. "Sure, man. Let's go."

Blackie and I follow Grimsby into the heavy surf, which is muddy from tearing up the beach. Each swell towers above us. No fear, no fear, I say to myself and keep my eyes on Blackie.

A huge swell rises above us. "Let's go!" I call to Blackie, but the dog is still nosing seaward.

"Hey, enough!" If there's a bigger wave out there, I don't want to face it. Even this one is too scary, but I'm stroking for it and committed and ready for the drop, which looks about fifteen feet. No backing out now. I spring to my feet and drop in.

KER-ASH! The wave closes down, bites into the shore. I'm tumbled in a wash of grit, like I've fallen into a cement mixer. The surf pounds me into the sand, scrapes me raw, then tosses me onto the beach, inches from a jagged bed of rock.

I struggle to my feet to see Grimsby and Blackie smoothly riding a mammoth crest. It had probably peaked a good fifty yards beyond the usual surf line.

Grimsby cuts back and heads toward me, finishing with a graceful floater over the foam. "What happened, man? Thought you were with us."

I shrug and look blank, hoping Grimsby hasn't seen me get tossed into the rinse cycle. My big chance to prove myself—I've blown it.

Blackie skids into the shore, dashes over, and woofs at me, as if to say, "Next time stick with me, grommet."

And I say, "Gotcha, boy."

Grimsby's looking seaward, timing the sets, figuring when to head out again.

I'm dying to say, "Gotta go," but that would make me look like a wuss. So I'm doomed to at least another hour of getting thrashed. Serves me right. I wanted to surf with the big guys.

Following Blackie's lead, Grimsby and I paddle out again. Blackie passes one, two, three swells. We keep moving over small swells, until we're more than a hundred yards out. Blackie starts paddling in a circle, like he's waiting. Waiting for what? A swell that crested out here would have to be a tidal wave.

Grimsby smiles. "Blackie seems to know what he's doing." Meaning, this time, stick with us.

What else can I do?

We rest on our boards for a while, till Blackie lets out a small yip and starts paddling toward shore.

Sure enough, a monstrous swell is heading toward us, I mean humongous.

We follow Blackie, paddling at an arm-killing pace. And all of a sudden, I feel a giant hand pick up my board, and I'm staring down at a valley of water at least twenty feet below me. Whoa! But Blackie's right next to me, enjoying the ride.

Lucky for us, the monster wave doesn't break. We ride along smoothly on the crest, and I see Grimsby get to his feet. I do the same.

And we ride. And ride. And ride some more, with the break following about twenty-five feet behind us. We see guys abandon their boards to dive through. We see others get eaten. And the rest standing on the shore watching our insane wave.

I'm able to hang in to the end. Grimsby and I skid to a stop in two feet of water, and he gives me a high five, in front of the other guys.

"You're new around here, right?" he says, as we park our boards for a rest. "Where you been surfing?"

I tell him I'm from L.A., that I usually surfed in Santa Monica, then I name drop a few spots like Zuma Beach and Trestles. It turns out he knows Skip's brother. "You surf with Hughie Short? I've gone against him in the eighteen-and-unders. The guy rips." He seems sort of impressed, so I tell him how hard Hughie used to work Skip and me.

"It shows," says Grimsby. He's quiet for a minute, then turns and squints at me. "Why don't you sign up for the November grom-fest?"

I shrug.

"Ever been in a contest?"

When I say no, he says, "I could give you a few tips."

The big Grimsby coaching me? Come on! Before I can answer he says, "You have a nice smooth style and rad maneuvers. With a little work you could own that mene-hunes division!"

"Oh." I feel my face turn purple. Menehunes division is for kids under eight.

"Whatsa matter? You don't dig competition?"

"Sure. I mean . . . it's just that . . . I happen to be eleven."

"Sorry." Grimsby's grin covers his gaffe. "No problem. You'll do fine in Boys'. That's twelve and under." But he didn't sound too sure.

The next morning I dash downstairs to get the paper, but as I pass through the kitchen, I see good dog Blackie trot it in, as usual, and drop it at Dad's feet.

I help myself to pancakes and wait for the explosion. I should have told my folks the whole story, but I knew they'd have a cow.

Dad holds up the paper. "What the . . . ? What's this?"

"No big deal," I say.

Dad reads about the rescue to Mom. Below the picture of Blackie and me, a caption reads "Heroic Dog."

Mom's speechless, except for "Son?"

A ten-inch story tells about the marooning, and ends with the capsized boat. "Grimsby and Fox waited for a break in the surf, then paddled uninjured to shore."

"It was no big deal," I keep saying. "The *Tribune*'s hard up for news."

Mom looks slightly dazed. "I'd say Blackie saved your life."

Dad growls at me. "Pete, what'd we tell you about surfing alone?"

"I wasn't surfing. I was sleeping."

"On the rock?"

"Yep."

"And *like* a rock, I guess." Dad tears out the article and puts it in his briefcase. "Well, be more careful next time"—he chuckles—"about where you take a nap."

Blackie sits next to my chair, his eyes following my bites of pancake from plate to mouth. He doesn't beg, just looks interested.

"Fine way to treat a hero," says Mom.

"*You* made the rule," I say. "No feeding at the table."

Mom leaves the breakfast room and a minute later she brings in a bowl of warmed beef kidney. "Just this once," she says.

While Blackie bolts his treat, Mom blows on her bangs and gives me a sad, serious look. "You know, Pete, soccer's a lot safer."

She'll never, never understand.

5 Blackie's Halloween

The following Friday is Halloween. Palm trees that line the beach look like black paper cutouts against the bright orange sunset. A change to Standard Time has shrunk the afternoon. The surfers are packing their boards when it's barely five o'clock.

Blackie and I take one last ride on a small but well-shaped wave. Blackie reaches the beach first and shakes his powerful body, pelting droplets on the surfers, who are standing in a group on the sand. The guys laugh; they like my dog a lot, probably more than they like me.

I work the white water to shore, jump off my board, then whistle to Blackie and head for my bike.

As I pass the lifeguard stand, I can hear the guys making plans for tonight's barbecue. Lozano asks, "What time's everyone showing?"

"Soon as I figure out a costume," says Grimsby.

"Soon as I can get a date," says Smart Marty, the goofy foot. Everyone laughs.

I keep on walking, not looking their way.

"See ya tomorrow?" calls Grimsby.

"Sure thing," I say.

Voices call from the group. "So long." "See ya, Pete."

I try not to feel left out. Since Grimsby's given me the thumbs-up, the guys are friendly enough, in a big brother sort of way. But everyone fades when the sun goes down.

"I should get real, huh, Blackie?" He looks up to let me know he's listening. "These guys are in high school. Grimsby's graduated. They don't want to hang out with kids like us. Or like me, anyway." I wonder how old in dog years Blackie is.

Mark Brill, a rich kid from my class, is giving a party, too. I heard Ben Kerr and Kevin Lee talking about it today in the cafeteria line. Even though I could walk home for lunch, Mom makes me stay at school "to make friends." I really dread noon hour.

Kerr says, "I'm coming as a monster."

"Who isn't?" says Lee.

But when I join them at the table, I see Lee nudge Kerr, and the talk of wigs and face paint changes to "Who's driving us to the game tomorrow?"

When Blackie and I get home, Mom's frosting a pumpkin layer cake. The kitchen smells of nutmeg and cinnamon. I'm starving. "Umm, thanks!"

"Sorry, hon. The Murrays are having a potluck."

"Uh, okay."

"Your dad and I are going as space aliens. We're painting ourselves green."

"Uh-huh." Right now I don't need a green face to feel like an alien.

Mom finishes with the orange frosting and starts painting jack-o'-lantern eyes with melted chocolate. "So, what's up? Have plans for the evening?"

"Nope."

"Oh. You could trick-or-treat around the neighborhood," says Mom.

"Who with?"

"With *whom*?" says the grammar teacher.

"Besides, trick or treat's for babies."

"Oh."

I hate Mom's little round "Oh"s. They can sting like BB shots; I know they mean she's disappointed. That's the worst part of not having friends: the way my folks worry about me, like I'm a geek or something.

With a few more swipes, she finishes the pumpkin face. But she's not quite finished with me. "Thought any more about going out for soccer?"

I open the freezer, take out some *taquitos*. "Yup." I've thought about it. That's about all.

"It would help you, you know, to—"

"You know how I feel about team sports." I pop the

taquitos into the toaster oven. "Everyone's too much into winning."

"So what's wrong with winning?"

"Nothing. It's when you don't win. Or you flub. Everyone gets on your case like it's a major disaster."

"I see."

"Surfers compete only with themselves. No pain. You win every time you rip a wave apart."

"I see." But I know she doesn't.

When the *taquitos* are crisp, I heap them with salsa and sour cream. I say between bites, "Maybe Blackie and I will hand out treats."

"Great idea." Mom seems relieved. Her son has a Plan. "Why don't you go pick up something?" She opens her kitchen desk and pulls out a twenty. "Be sure to get the wrapped candies."

"Yup."

"But not the big ones."

"Uh-huh."

"You can pick up a burger or something." She eyes my *taquitos.* "Or is that your dinner?"

"One of them," I say.

At the supermarket all the candy is marked down. So are the sleazy kid costumes and masks, the false noses and teeth. I look out through the glass door of the market, where two little kids, in cheesecloth skeleton costumes, are petting Blackie. That gives me an idea.

Back home I set my packages in the kitchen. I tell Blackie, "Tonight I'm gonna make you a star."

He wags his tail; he'd like that.

I finish carving a pumpkin and stick one of Mom's bayberry candles inside. I pour a few sacks of wrapped candies into a basket. From another market bag I pull out a long scraggly gray wig and a pointed witch's hat.

I put the wig on Blackie's head, then tie on the witch's hat. Blackie shakes his head a couple of times but doesn't complain.

"Here, boy." I lead witch Blackie to the front porch, command him to sit and stay, then put the lighted pumpkin down in front of him.

Back inside, I close the door and peek through the window to watch the action.

Before long the whole neighborhood knows about the black witch on the porch. Trick-or-treaters come by the dozens: Tinkerbells, superheroes, aliens—and a bunch of monsters. Witch Blackie eyes them, curious. Sometimes he thumps his tail, but he never leaves his post.

"Hey, this is the coolest!" The voice on the porch is none other than Mark Brill, dressed as Count Dracula. Easy to spot through the makeup, he's the tallest guy in the class and the only one whose voice is changing. A half-dozen ghosts and ghouls have followed him up the walk. The last kids have left the door open; it's too late for me to hide.

"Trick or treee-at!" Brill holds out his pillowcase. In spite of his height, the tuxedo is three sizes too big, and it looks sort of strange with his air-cushioned Doc Martens. He looks stunned as he faces me. "Well, hi, Pete. Whatcha doing here?"

"Uh . . ." How to answer his stupid question? "This is my house."

"No lie? And your witch pooch?"

"Yup."

"Hey guys, look who's—"

"Hey, Pete." More guys, most of them unrecognizable mummies and vampires, file onto the porch, carrying large sacks, even a couple of trash bags.

Blackie remains sitting, but uses a hind leg to scratch his back. Probably the long gray wig is tickling him.

"Witch got an itch?" says Lee, a Frankenstein. The group hoots.

"Let's see the treats," says Brill.

Some nerve. Leave me out of the party, then come here for refreshments. But with a dozen guys on the porch, I'm not about to argue. "Come on in. Help yourself." I hold out the basket of candies.

All those polite little Tinkerbells and cowboys, with their parents watching, have taken one or two pieces and said, "Thank you." Now these guys grab fistfuls, leaving just a couple of caramels in the basket.

"Take it easy," I say, but try to sound friendly. "It's only seven o'clock. I've gotta—"

"Looks like you'd better close down," says Brill. "Why don't you come out with us?"

"Naw, I have to—"

"We're going to bag a ton of candy, then go to my house for Kentucky Fried and stuff. Got a couple of real scary videos. . . ."

"Uh, I don't have a costume." Lame excuse, but I'm not about to jump at his offer.

"What you talking about?" says Brill. "Your dog's got the best getup of all." He won't look at me, starts messing with his cummerbund. "We just thought up this gig today. Didn't see you around after school. . . ."

"I surf after school," I say, to help the lie along.

Brill whips a flip phone from his jacket pocket and speed-dials his mom. "One more coming, okay?"

I wait to be urged a little more, then leave a note on the kitchen counter, and grab a jacket, along with Blackie's leash. Before I blow out the pumpkin candle, I signal Blackie to "beg nice" on his hind legs, then stick a broom in his paws. One of the monsters snaps a picture. The ghosts and ghouls cheer. "Really cool dog," says Brill.

Right. And where, and who, would I be without him?

The next morning I'm in my wet suit by 7:30. Hunched over the kitchen table, I shovel in granola. Blackie, in the laundry room, is wolfing down his kibble.

Mom nibbles on a banana, part of the amazing fruit diet she saw in a magazine. "What's the big hurry?"

"The ocean's blue glass this morning. Want to hit it before the wind comes up."

"Have fun last night?"

"It was okay."

"Just okay?"

"Sort of fun, I guess."

"Oh?"

"We watched videos, so I didn't talk to too many guys. Besides, with all the costumes, I didn't know who was who."

Another "Oh."

"But Blackie was a big hit. I dressed him up like a witch."

Mom smiles into her sliced kiwi.

"It's only because of Blackie I got invited."

"Come on, Pete."

"True." I tell her how Brill and the guys came to meet the witch on the porch. "So what could he do but invite me?"

"He didn't *have* to."

I don't answer. We can hear Blackie's dog tag clinking against his bowl. After a while I say what Mom wants to hear. "Brill wants to go surfing with me."

"That's great!"

"Not great. He's pretty much a beginner."

"Pete, give the guy a chance, will you?"

"Probably a sponger."

"A what?"

"You know. Rides a foam boogie board."

"Oh, stop that!" She shakes her head, then finishes off

the banana in one bite. "Pete, why are you so . . . so . . . standoffish?"

"I'm training. For contests. Don't have time to fool around with some speed bump."

"You could use a friend."

I whistle; Blackie leaves his bowl and skids across the kitchen floor. "*Here's* my friend."

"You rely too much on that dog."

"We'll be home for lunch." I bang the screen door. And hope that I won't run into Brill at the beach. I don't have time to teach the guy to stand up on a real surfboard.

Sure, I could use a friend. Maybe later. But right now, I've got a contest to win.

6 Grounding Swells

November brings radical waves from the Alaska storms. I've spent every afternoon at Main Beach. When the surfers come to shore for a breather, there isn't a guy in the crowd who doesn't come up to pet Blackie. "Hey, there's our hero. Surfer Dog!"

Blackie loves the attention. He shows off by tearing up and down the beach, ending in a skid before the group.

I pretty much stick with Blackie's lead. By this time I'm sure it's not my imagination. He really does have this weird instinct—ask anybody—about which waves give the longest ride. To tell the truth, even the better surfers have begun to follow Blackie. I see them watching, checking, without letting on. I guess you'd say Blackie's become the surfers' mascot.

They sort of treat me like a mascot, too. I try to act as friendly as Blackie, do everything but wag my butt. And as long as I know my place—stay out of the way, keep my mouth shut—I'm welcome on Main Beach.

Grimsby, as promised, has begun helping me get ready for the Fall All-County contest. With just locals entering, I may actually have a chance. But Grimsby's on my case like I'm going for the World Cup. "Be yourself. Develop your own style. And relax. Get loose!"

Sure, get loose. Improvise. Not so easy with all those hotshots watching.

But, like Grimsby says, "You want to ride the big ones, you gotta pay your dues."

I've been paying my dues all right, with gallons of salt water up the nose. But never mind the wipeouts; I know I'm getting better.

Friday Blackie and I come home sandy and dripping as usual. I'm rinsing my feet and Blackie's paws with the hose. Mom leans out the back door. She does not look happy.

"I had a conference with your teacher today."

"Oh?" I forget to breathe.

"What do you have to say for yourself?"

No answer. I wait until Blackie and I are in the kitchen. "Umm, smells good."

"Beef stew." She drops some potatoes into the pot. "What do you have to say . . . ?"

"Did all my homework." I open the refrigerator.

"Don't spoil your dinner."

I pour a glass of milk, palm some oatmeal cookies from the jar, and sit at the kitchen table. "Turned in my book reports."

"Late," says Mom. "All marked down to C because of lateness."

From the pocket of her jeans she pulls an evaluation form. She reads:

> *"I believe Peter is very bright, but he is not working up to his potential. He gazes out the window, with his mind somewhere else. His home assignments show comprehension of the subject but are executed with haste."*

She sticks the report under a magnet on the refrigerator door. "You *are* bright."

I shake my head. "I don't know what Mrs. Blaine is talking about half the time."

"Because you're not listening."

Blackie noses me; he can probably smell the trouble. I smooth his ears. "Math and history are boring."

"I know where your head is most of the time." Chop, chop, she dices some carrots. "It's diving through some wave."

I keep stroking Blackie's ears. What's to say?

"Sorry, son. I can't let this pass." Chop, chop. "I'm going to have to ground you until your work improves."

I bam my fist on the table. The milk jumps. "No way!"

"From three-thirty on you'll stay in your room. And work." She tosses the carrots into the stew.

"But Mom, I've *gotta* surf!"

"You heard me!"

"It's only two weeks till the fall contest. Grimsby's knocking himself out to help me. You've gotta let me practice, Mom. You don't know—"

"I'll talk to your father," she says.

I spend a long night, rolling over and pounding my pillow. With each turn I wake Blackie, who sleeps with his chin on my shins. Earlier I could hear my parents in their bedroom, discussing their problem son. So what's the big deal? I've never had trouble in school before. It's just that Mrs. Blaine is so boring. She even bores herself, I swear— yawns between every sentence. One morning I counted seventeen.

At breakfast Dad doesn't even taste his coffee, gets right to the point. "You're grounded until further notice."

"So how long is that?"

"We'll keep in touch with Mrs. Blaine."

"Mrs. Lame Blaine."

"Watch it," Dad barks.

Mom speaks oh so sweetly. "We'll make an exception for the day of the surfing contest."

"Thanks a bunch. Great chance I'll have, with no practice."

Blackie whimpers; he knows what's going on. "Not fair,

is it, boy?" More whimpers. "It's not fair to punish Black-ie. He needs his exercise."

"Blackie will do just fine. He loves going shopping."

"He's a surfer, not a shopper."

Dad reaches out and grabs my arm. "Any more lip from you, Pete, and you won't surf till Christmas."

7 Sneakers

Now it's Saturday; the sea's hot and glassy with a pumping swell, corduroy to the horizon. And here I am, filling in a map of Africa.

Blackie is lying under my desk. Now and then he gets up, stretches, and goes out on the deck of my bedroom. He's looking down at the coastline, three blocks away. Once in a while his eyes follow a flight of gulls. Then he comes back and settles at my feet. He looks up at me, as if to ask, "Hey, boss, when are we hitting the beach?"

Mom and Dad have gone to play tennis and have lunch at the club with friends. They didn't say when they'd be back—probably on purpose.

I take a razor-point pen and begin marking: Algeria, Libya, Egypt. My folks don't realize how lucky they are. I've been a pretty good kid, never lied, except for a fib now and then, never stole anything, never cut school. Never touched a cigarette, let alone the other stuff.

Ethiopia, Kenya, Somalia.

Around lunchtime the phone rings; I go to my folks' bedroom to answer.

It's Grimsby. "Hey, where are you? We have work to do."

"Can't make it. Uh, have stuff to do around the house."

"This afternoon, then?"

I can't tell Grimsby I've been grounded, like some balky kid.

"Nope, gotta go somewhere. For the weekend."

"Okay, Monday for sure." The guy wasn't going to let go.

I look down at the open datebook on Mom's desk, one of those museum calendars with a painting on every page. Monday afternoon (van Gogh's *Starry Night*) had an arrow through it, 1:00 to 5:00 P.M., where Mom had written "Book Club."

"Great. Meet you at Main after school."

After I put down the phone, I check Mom's appointments. Tuesday (*Sunflowers*) 4:00 P.M. "Dentist." And after that is scrawled, "Vote!" A good hour and a half.

Wednesday, 3:00 P.M. "Aggie, tennis." Aggie's Mom's partner for ladies' doubles. Two hours easy.

So far we're looking good. Mom probably won't be taking Blackie.

Thursday morning is marked "Hospital"; Mom's a Pink Lady volunteer. The afternoon is blank, except for "Water African violets." But I know that on Thursday afternoons Mom hits the supermarket, then goes to the open air farmers' market. Couldn't possibly be home before dark.

Friday afternoon is also blank, except for "Pick up cleaning." On Fridays Mom usually goes into Dad's law office, fools around with the books, and takes his checks to the bank.

I see myself in the bureau mirror, bent over the desk like a crook planning a bank job. Blackie's watching me, looking serious. "Pretty sneaky, huh, boy?" He still looks solemn. "But haven't they forced me into it?"

The dog nods.

"This time they've gone too far—trashing my surfing. If they only knew how I've been busting my butt."

Blackie wags his tail; he totally agrees.

I flip some more through the calendar, make notes, then get back to the map. I'd better get cracking on the books. Looks like I'll have to stay up a few nights.

On Monday I dash home from school, and Blackie's waiting, all yelps and waggles. Mom has left a note on the kitchen table. "Home around 5:15. Lemon bars in the microwave. I'm hiding them from the ants."

Is this a trap? Isn't she going to call and check up? Maybe my folks *do* trust me. I scoop out a row of lemon bars, then dive into my wet suit. I take the phone off the hook, just in case. If Mom calls and gets a busy signal, I can always say I was working on a project with someone. Which, in a way, I am. Call it oceanography.

We find Grimsby in the surf at the south end of Main Beach. This part of the shoreline has been carved away by heavy waves. There are wide patches of rock where, in the summer, there were stretches of white sand.

The surfers have begun moving north, beyond Mouse Rock, where there's a good reef break. Grimsby and I can have this beach pretty much to ourselves. Which is probably just as well, if he's going to yell at me.

Led by Blackie, we plunge through the shallow surf and head out beyond the breakline. November's waves can be scary; it takes nerve to face the big ones. But Blackie, as usual, is completely fearless.

I check my watch a lot and take one last ride at ten minutes of five. Blackie and I race home, and while I'm dressing I run Mom's hair dryer over his coat. I finish tumble-drying the wet suit just as her car pulls in. Phew! I don't need this.

The next afternoon, I'm still in my wet suit when Mom comes home. "Forgot my sample ballot," she calls. "Where are you, dear?"

I dash for the bathroom and pull Blackie in behind me, locking the door. "In here." I turn the water on full force.

"You're taking a bath? What's the matter? Are you sick?" I haven't taken a bath since my rubber fleet gave out.

"Tub's a fun place to read. Mrs. Blaine even says so." Mrs. Blaine. That was a stroke of genius.

"I like it myself. I'll hand in my bubble bath if you want."

"Mo-om!"

"Blackie in there? I thought he might like a ride downtown."

"He's all wet."

"You're taking a bath with the dog? That's gross."

I didn't lie. Blackie *is* wet. Also salty.

"Okay, dear. I'll see you after five."

My hand trembles as I turn off the water. It's going to be a long three weeks.

8 Contest Time

Mid-November brings dark skies and frequent rainstorms. Although the beach is still sandy, several drainage creeks, which carry the runoff from cloudbursts, now cut through the shoreline.

While the soccer players have been forced indoors by the rains, the surfers are out full force. Each day I check in at home, lay out my books, check Mom's calendar, then sneak out to meet Grimsby for his daily coaching.

Grimsby's been pretty patient, but sometimes he loses it. "Whatsa matter. You chicken? Wait for the big one!"

"But that one looked—"

"When in doubt, paddle out," says Grimsby. "Like Blackie does."

"Blackie doesn't have a board to worry about."

Sometimes I get tired of having my timing compared with Blackie's. I've tried to make ride decisions without watching him, but a lot of times I blow it. Sometimes I wonder if, without my surfer dog, I'd make any kind of showing.

The contest is set for the Saturday after Thanksgiving. That day when I wake up, little frogs are doing the *macarena* in my stomach. What have I gotten myself into?

Like I told Mom, a surfer competes only with himself. But now look at me, with a full case of the shakes. Why did I suddenly get so hot to go up against the rest? And not just to compete. To bury them!

Mom calls with a cheery voice, "Cranberry muffins— hurry!" She's been extra nice these past few weeks, probably feels guilty for grounding me. Which makes me feel super-guilty for sneaking out on her.

A couple of times I've had to steal downstairs after dinner, make double-strong instant coffee, and hit the books till midnight. It's been worth it, though; Lame Blaine has actually come through with a couple of B's and an A-minus. So, as of today, no more sneaking. I'm free to surf again.

In the kitchen Mom puts a half grapefruit in front of me. "Want eggs, cereal?"

"Not hungry."

"You need to keep your energy up." She cracks an egg into the frying pan. "What time should we be there?"

"You and Dad really want to come?" I've sort of been hoping they wouldn't show, in case I flop.

"Your first contest? Of course!"

"Twelve and under go on around noon."

"Great! I'll pack a picnic. Fix some turkey sandwiches, make some potato salad . . ."

At the thought of my folks watching, the frogs in my belly start their dance again.

A ribbon of cars lines the shore along Main Beach. Surfers from towns throughout the county are arriving to compete, shouting to old pals, huddling in groups to catch up on the tides and the weather and who's ripping.

Wavelengths, one of the local surf shops, has put up a hot-pink judges' tent, with gigantic speakers blasting surf tunes like "Barrel Blues." Inside the tent are free snacks and drinks for contestants, plus a tableful of trophies and a stack of T-shirt prizes. At the sight of the prize table, I feel my blood temperature drop about twenty degrees. A surfer only competes with himself. Sure thing.

I sit with Grimsby and some other surfers to watch the first heat, for the menehunes. One of them, a little towhead, is only five years old. Grimsby points out the errors and fills me in on how to best handle today's surf, heavy but choppy.

The menehunes' heat ends, with the five-year-old one of the two high scorers. The winner is Patches Pauley, a wiry seven-year-old from Crystal Bay who's developed maneuvers that would be hard to ignore.

The loudspeaker calls for the boys' division surfers to report and pick up their shirts. Over their wet suits contestants wear bright Lycra jerseys, which identify them by color. I'm given blue, which suits my mood. Why am I torturing myself with this crazy competition?

"Stay cool," says Grimbsy. "You'll do fine."

"*We'll* do fine." Blackie follows me into the surf.

"No way," says Grimsby. "Blackie didn't sign up."

"You're kidding. But I can't—"

He shakes his head. "No dogs allowed."

I spot my folks settling into their sand chairs and take Blackie to them. Mom has two picnic baskets. Dad has his binoculars and camcorder. Maybe they're getting into surfing after all.

I explain to them about the contest. Heats for each division last fifteen minutes. Surfers are graded on their best three waves. There are four riders in each heat; the best two will advance to the quarterfinals.

Dad says, "Go for it!"

Mom ties Blackie's leash to the sand chair and says, "Cowabunga!" which is the only surfing word she knows. I take off with my board.

I paddle out beyond the surf line and wait on my board for the blast of the air horn. Looking back at Mom and Dad, I see Blackie, alert on his haunches, between them. Blackie is beached. I'm on my own. And I'm scared.

The horn blasts. As I watch the waves roll toward me, I try to pretend I'm Blackie. Shall I catch the first wave of the set, or wait for a better chance?

I pass up a good-sized wave and stroke out to meet the

next one. It's a clean four-footer with a big open face—gives me plenty of room for a couple of quick slashes and a full roundhouse cutback into the whitewater. Just show me two more like that!

The wind picks up, the sea surface grows rougher, but by waiting longer than I think I should, I manage to grab another left, which I ride backside with a few backhand lip smacks.

Take it easy. With two good scores behind me, I can afford to hang out a few minutes, take a breather, wait for just the right shape. "When in doubt, paddle out."

But the set has ended. Now I drift over mush that breaks with a hiss against the shore. I check my watch. Four minutes to go. I'd better move toward shallower water, catch whatever is available. Shoot, is that what Blackie would do?

I skid across a couple of three-footers but can't manage much footwork; the force just isn't there.

Finally, with one minute to go, I see what I've been waiting for, a great peak coming from the south, about twenty feet away. I make a dash for it, barely make the drop, and hang on through a critical section. I end up getting shot out onto the shoulder, where I can kick out just before the super-shallow area known as the boneyard.

Mom and Dad clap and call out. Blackie strains on his leash and barks, his tail wagging. Grimsby comes up with a toothy smile. "Nice going. You've made the quarters."

"Nothing to it."

I introduce Grimsby to my folks, who are already into the lunch. Blackie nuzzles me but keeps his eyes on the turkey sandwiches.

"You've got an okay surfer here," says Grimsby.

Mom says, "Pretty radical. With all those big tubes!" I wish she'd stick with "Cowabunga!"

"We're really proud of him," says Dad.

"Should be. This guy's a goer." He claps me around the shoulders. "He's been out here working his tail off every afternoon."

Mom looks from Grimsby to me, then over to Dad, whose expression is hidden by his cap and sunglasses.

"How about a sandwich?" she asks.

9 Water on the Brain

Mom passes the potato salad and pickles in near silence, humming an unrecognizable tune.

"Yeah, let's see you drill 'em this afternoon," says Grimsby. "You have a good chance." He hasn't a clue about the problem he's caused. He scarfs the lunch while I nibble on a pickle.

Mom and Dad finish their sandwiches, pack up the lunch, and don't even offer the pie. "Sorry, we can't stay." Mom's voice is as cool and flat as washed sand. "I forgot. I'm supposed to help at the art show today." Dad says not one word as they fold their sand chairs and fade, taking Blackie with them.

As I watch them leave, my legs turn to wet spaghetti and stay that way. I blow the second heat big time and am given a consolation prize—a black T-shirt printed with Blackbeard Surfwear's skull and bones.

I'm wearing the T-shirt as I sit on the sofa in the family

room, facing Mom and Dad. Its death symbol seems right on. The two perch on the edge of their wing-back chairs. Blackie sits between them, making it seem like three against one.

A fire flickers in the grate, casting shadows across Dad's sour face. The Lakers game is on the TV behind me, with the sound off. I can see Dad's eyes follow the players as he says, "You're grounded until Christmas."

Mom says, "It just kills me that we can't trust you."

I signal to Blackie; I need someone on my side. Over he comes and lies at my feet, head between paws.

"You don't get it, Mom. I *have* to surf. It's not like I *wanted* to sneak out."

Dad tucks his chin down like a sitcom dad. "You don't have to surf, and you're not going to surf."

"Grounding. Geez, can't you guys figure out something more original?"

"We are not *guys*," says Mom.

I move to the floor and hug my knees, trying to keep myself together. "I could work, maybe, like prisoners do. Clean the garage, pull weeds, and stuff."

"I could use some help around the house," says Mom.

Dad looks at her and shrugs.

I sit up and smile. "Thanks, Dad. I'll work hard."

Dad nods. "But you're still grounded till Christmas."

I stare down at the skull and bones on my chest. Twenty-five days in the graveyard.

· · ·

After the punishment tasks are finished, Blackie and I spend most afternoons in my room, or on the deck staring down at the beach. I snitch Dad's binoculars from the hall closet; on clear days I can make out who the surfers are. There goes Grimsby. Whoops, missed, too far out. Here comes Smart Marty, the goofy foot, pulling into a grinding right-hand closeout. Lozano lands an aerial fakey and straightens out in the whitewater.

"Shoot!" I take my half-dozen pillows and chuck them at the window. "I'm gonna forget everything I've learned."

Blackie knows how bummed I am. He comes over and rubs against me, and looks up as if to say, "We'll think of something."

The next day on the way home from school, I stop at the library and check out three surfing videos. I carry them home in my backpack and wait until Mom has gone on errands.

As soon as Mom's car pulls out, I get my skateboard from the garage and set it down in front of the family room VCR. Then with the tape rolling, I practice turns along with the surfing greats who are dropping into twenty-footers on the north shore of Oahu, Hawaii. I *have* to stay in shape.

Blackie loves the tapes. He circles in front of the TV, barking, as I do my practice turns. One, two, three, whack off the lip. This is working out great. I'm going with the flow. Now shift and turn and . . .

CRASH! The board shoots out from under me and

topples a ginger-jar lamp. I conk my head on the coffee table and lie dazed on the carpet, seeing circles and stars.

Through them appears the face of Mom. It is not a smiley face.

Mom passes the salad to Dad. "What are we going to do with him?" When my folks are mad, they talk as if their evil son were someplace else.

Dad heaps his plate with broccoli and tomatoes. "I tell you, the kid is obsessed."

I make a mental note to look the word up after dinner. I've heard of people who are *possessed* by evil spirits. Is that what Dad means?

"I have some money saved," I say. "I'll pay for the lamp."

"I bought that jar on our honeymoon in Hong Kong," says Mom. "We can't get another."

"I'm sorry, Mom. I really am."

More than sorry. Maybe I'm obsessed or possessed or whatever. Things are going from bad to worse.

The binoculars are discovered and locked in the trunk of Dad's car, along with the skateboard. Dad's also snipped the cord of the TV set and bought one of those clamp-on plugs, which he carries in his briefcase.

School is a drag, with all the guys either playing soccer or talking about it. Brill asks a couple of times, "When can we catch some waves?" but I put him off with limp excuses—a knee injury, blown-out surf.

Besides being tall and rich, Brill is also a brain. He might not understand someone being grounded for grades. After the second turndown, he shrugs and says, "You let me know, okay?"

Except for Blackie, my life is a total zero. But even Blackie seems changed—kind of bored and whiny. Every time he hears car keys rattle, he dashes to Mom or Dad to beg for a ride. Who can blame him?

I have to call Grimsby, tell him about my grounding. He just laughs and says, "Yeah, I've been there." And a second later he says, "There's worse things."

I ask him like what.

"Watching your pals go off to U.C. in La Jolla or Santa Barbara while you're stuck in Community College." He's talking about himself.

Then he says to me, "The guys really miss Blackie. How about I take him out with me afternoons?"

"Thanks, but . . ."

I think about my dog, pacing the bedroom, staring off the deck at the ocean. I remember what I said to Mom: "It's not fair to punish Blackie." My throat aches, but I answer, "Sure. Nice of you to offer."

Now, in my bedroom prison, with Mom's nautical decorating and all those surfing posters, I don't even have my surfer dog for company. At first, I'd gaze off the deck, trying to figure which one of the black dots on the ocean was Blackie's head. But now I just pull down the blinds.

I have no choice but to read or study or go loony. Might

as well get ahead on the book reports. At the school library I check out *Captains Courageous* and *Treasure Island* and *The Cay*. Funny how all the books I choose have to do with the ocean. Dad would probably say I have water on the brain.

Maybe that's my problem.

10 A Sad Discovery

The day after Christmas, I get up at sunrise. Free at last! From my window I can see a pink glow tinting the glassy sea. I whisper to Blackie, "We're out of here!"

Mrs. Blaine called Mom on Christmas Eve to say that I'd "improved noticeably" both in "performance and attitude." Now, while school's out, I can spend all day, every day, on the beach with Blackie.

On goes the wet suit, first time in nearly a month. It seems shorter and tighter, and the torn spot at the ankle needs some neoprene cement. I asked for a new wet suit for Christmas, but instead got a pair of in-line skates and a basketball hoop. My folks' message comes through loud and clear.

Christmas has brought a break in the northwestern storms. Today the sky is full of puffy clouds, and the hills are covered with green. The air smells fresh and earthy.

With Blackie bounding alongside, I ride my bike down

Ocean Avenue and park it near the north end of town. I can't wait for that first chilly plunge, and watch Blackie streak through the water ahead of me.

With most of the shoreline chewed up by storms, the surfers have moved even farther from Main Beach, almost to the end of the cove. Blackie and I make our way through the sand dunes toward the gully where Chumash Creek empties into the ocean.

The tide is out, and the creek water has fanned out over the beach; it sparkles in the sunlight. A flock of gulls is feeding in a shallow lagoon to the side of the creek.

Beyond the lagoon a drainage culvert empties into the creek. Blackie sees it and takes off. He loves exploring dark places like caves and tunnels. He races ahead, then stops to drink the water that's spilling from the culvert.

"No, boy!" I catch up with him. "If you're thirsty . . ." I nudge Blackie's head and point him toward the fresh water upstream.

He stops to sniff beside the culvert. A small metal object. He noses the ground and uncovers a strap.

I lean down and pick it up. A leather collar. A dog collar. Blackie sniffs and whimpers.

The tag is inscribed MACKIE, and there's a telephone number.

"Mackie?" I say.

Blackie barks.

"Mackie?"

He barks again.

On the way home from the beach I try several commands. No question, Blackie answers to both names.

In the shower I strip off my wet suit. The dog collar falls from my sleeve onto the tile. I pick it up and read the phone number again: 805-555-1192. The number of Blackie's master. Or Mackie's.

Water streams into my eyes as I stare at the numbers. The area code is the same as the one for Whaler's Cove. But the prefix numbers are different. All Whaler's Cove numbers begin with 995. Blackie probably lived in a town somewhere down the coast. *If* Blackie is really Mackie. Only a slim chance, I tell myself, and tell myself again.

I turn off the shower and wrap myself in a towel, go to my bedroom dresser drawer, and drop the collar into a carved wooden box of my private stuff: some moonstones, a Chumash arrowhead, a couple of feathers from Blue Boy, my long-gone cockatoo.

Lying back on the bed, I look up at my surfing posters. The house is quiet; I can hear the rattle of the ice maker downstairs in the kitchen. Mom has taken Blackie to the pet store to buy some new kibble. Pet World is running a special this week: dogs can taste-test and pick their favorite flavors.

How am I going to tell Mom about the collar? Or am I? I can feel a dull ache in my stomach. It makes me feel hungry, even though I've just polished off two microwaved mini-pizzas.

I try not to think about what might happen—the rest

of my life surfing without Blackie. The whole rest of my life trying to sleep without that warm lump in my bed.

It's not fair. We tried our best to find Blackie's owner. That was months ago. By now his master has probably found another Labrador. He doesn't need two.

Major bummer. Why, of all the dogs in the world, did I have to meet up with a surfer dog?

The words hit me hard. Surfer dog. That owner could search the planet and never find another Blackie. He could buy a hundred Labradors; he'll never train another dog to catch the waves so perfectly.

I'll have to make that call.

I hear Mom down in the kitchen. Seconds later Blackie bounds up the stairs, comes to my bed, and nuzzles my towel. He's wearing a new wool plaid vest, with the price tag still on.

Better wait to tell Mom tomorrow.

"Mackie?" says Mom. "Sounds more like a Scotch terrier." But at the sound of the name Blackie stirs.

I'm sitting at the breakfast table, rubbing Blackie's head. So sleek. So silky. "Guess I'd better call."

"Finish your cereal," says Mom. "It'll get mushy."

I practically choke on each swallow, but I keep eating. I'm in no hurry to make that phone call. A few words and it's over for Blackie and me. Forever.

"Why not call this afternoon?" says Mom. "Give the girls a chance to say good-bye."

And the butcher and the baker and the postmaster, no doubt. Mom is taking the news hard. Her eyes are all misty.

I'm glad I waited until this morning to tell her about the collar. Otherwise she probably would have cried herself to sleep. Like I did.

"After all," she says, "we've had Blackie since September. Another day won't matter."

"I'd like to get it over with."

"If you say so," she says. "The man probably works. Couldn't come until tonight anyway."

"What makes you think the owner is a man?"

Mom leans down and hugs Blackie. "Just seems like a man's dog."

"Not around here, he doesn't."

I pick up the kitchen phone and take the dog tag from my pocket. My fingers fumble the numbers; I punch them again. Mom looks away and holds her hands over her ears.

There are four rings, then a recording. "The number you have reached has been disconnected."

11 Surfing the Big Time

Spring comes early. The days roll by in fast sets. I work like crazy every afternoon, getting ready for the Easter week surf meet. This is a Western Surfing Association meet; surfers from all over California will come to try for the division title and for computer rankings. All the big names will be there: Troy Hischer, Slider Vickery, and, best of all, Matt McCoy.

I've followed their heats in *Surfer* magazine, cut out their pictures, studied their moves. A poster of McCoy hangs on the wall opposite my bed.

On the day of the contest the town is jammed. People have been coming since sunup to stake out the best viewing spots.

Blackbeard Surfwear is sponsoring the day. They've put up a large black-and-white-striped judges' tent, strung with pennants of Blackbeard's skull and bones. A table in the Blackbeard tent holds trophies and gifts for the big winners. First prize for the boys' division is a new Black-beard zipperless wet suit. I need that suit; I can barely breathe in the old one.

I help Grimsby unload his Jeep, which is full of refreshments and minor prizes: T-shirts, caps, board wax—provided by Moondoggies Surf Shop, where he works part-time.

"You're sure quiet this morning, Pete," says Grimsby. "Almost as quiet as our surf."

"That's what I'm worried about," I tell him. "The ripples. I had a nightmare last night—about surfing a contest with no waves."

"You're not on till eleven or so," says Grimsby. "The swells should pick up with the incoming tide. But I feel sorry for the poor menehunes."

I set down a carton of hot dog buns next to the propane barbecue grill. "They say Patches Pauley had a birthday. He's moved up to boys."

"Got you worried?"

"Who needs to be outclassed by an eight-year-old?"

"Pauley's tough," says Grimsby. "Has firsts all over the state. The menehunes will be glad to get rid of him."

"Just what I need to hear."

"No problem, man. You've learned your timing from the greatest. The one and only . . . Surfer Dog!" He nods toward Blackie, who's sniffing from a polite distance the stack of uncooked franks.

"How'd you like to be me," says Grimsby, "coming up against McCoy?"

"You can do it," I sound sort of lame, like I'm not sure he can.

"The stakes are scary. I could get a sponsored world tour."

"You're ready for the big time." But I still don't sound convincing. Here I am, trying to prop up Grimsby. How old do you have to grow, how good do you have to get before you stop doubting yourself?

Grimsby's style is smooth and his moves radical; he's probably ready for a major win. But I'm not sure he can outclass the big McCoy.

Because of the crowds, the summer leash law is in force. When the setup is finished, I tether Blackie to a post behind the judges' tent. There's a golf tournament, so my folks won't be coming today. At least that's what they told me.

At the front of the tent I see Mark Brill and feel like ducking. I've meant to ask him to go surfing, but there just hasn't been time, what with meeting Grimsby every afternoon.

"So, Pete. How's it goin'?"

"Hey, Brill. What you doing here?" The guy couldn't be entering.

"Uh, I live here. This is sort of my front yard." He points to a large house to our left.

I feel like a dork. I'd been to his place on Halloween. "Right! I didn't recognize your place from the beach side."

"I watch you guys sometimes from my front window. You're rippin' lately, Pete."

"Thanks. I need that. A little nervous today."

Brill's cell phone rings. He answers, then says, "My breakfast's ready. What time's your heat?"

"Sometime before noon."

"I'll look for you."

I sit with Grimsby watching the menehunes struggle to ride on waves that are little more than streaks of foam. "Don't see that swell coming," I say.

The horn sounds, the P.A. calls the twelve and under to get ready. I pick up my Lycra jersey, a red one, and grab my board. Then I go rub Blackie's head for luck.

As I pass the Blackbeard tent, I spot that prize wet suit and feel my guts begin to knot. Why can't I surf like Blackie, just for the fun of it?

But Blackie doesn't need a wet suit. Or praise. Or honor. Or whatever it is that makes surfers enter contests.

The heat turns out not much better than my nightmare. There's Patches Pauley, practically doing the hula on top of every wave. And here I am, with a body that feels as if it's all bones, loosely tied together by a tight wet suit. Worse, my board seems to have grown a mind of its own.

Without Blackie leading the way, my timing is way off. Overanxious, I paddle for a small wave as a bigger one looms up behind it. Abandoning the first, I stroke to the outside for the bigger one, but it breaks in front of me.

Shoot, I've missed them both. I turn to see Patches's yellow board sending spray; he's caught the set wave and is milking it to shore right in front of the judges' stand.

Finally I get the feel of the board, catch a decent right, and hold my own with a couple of off-the-lips and a little snapback at the end. The horn blasts; time's up. I know I've done poorly. I scan the beach, hoping Brill hasn't been watching.

Grimsby comes out of the tent. He says to Patches, "Good going, grommet. You made it." Then he turns to me. "'S okay, dude. Lots of years to go."

"No chance. It's over. Competition's not for me."

Grimsby looks from me to Patches and back again. "Before you're ready to win, pal, you gotta learn how to lose."

I watch Patches bolt down two hot dogs while mine sits half eaten. Then Patches's Dad calls him out of the tent, poses him for a photo, like he's already won. Not to wish any bad luck, but I can't help hoping he'll drop the second round. Kids like that need to stay humble.

I'm glad my parents were busy. All those days of practice down the chute. An eight-year-old makes me look like dog meat.

It's almost time for the men's heat. Grimsby's gone up toward Mouse Rock to catch a couple before his heat. Now he's on his way back, walking with another surfer.

Whoa! Not just another surfer. The real Matt McCoy!

McCoy stands about six-foot-three, with streaked blond hair and a deep tan. He's walking in big long steps, looking, not cocky, but, let's say, confident, like the hotshot he is. The two are coming my way. I'm going to meet The Man.

From behind the tent, I hear Blackie whimper, then break into a loud bark. After I brought him the rest of my hot dog, he stretched out for a snooze. The gulls must have woken him up.

The barks gets louder, then turn into squeals. I head for the back of the tent. "Hey, boy, what's the matter?"

Blackie's leaping, straining against the leash.

"Stay, boy."

He goes on leaping and howling.

"Blackie, *stay*."

The dog doesn't hear me. He's going wild.

When I turn, I see the reason. Matt McCoy is running toward him, calling, "Mackie, Mackie! Is that you?"

12 That's All. Just "Woof."

I barely see the rest of the contest. The surfers streak by in a blur. I stare out to sea, with Blackie—or Mackie—beside me, held firmly by his leash. I barely notice when Patches, on his bright yellow board, takes the second round.

Blackie is quiet while the men's contestants battle through their heat. McCoy told him to sit and stay, and that was that. The master had spoken. Now the dog's eyes follow McCoy's every move as he glides through the waves.

For some reason—the dog, maybe?—McCoy is not up to his usual performance. In the semifinals he comes in third, letting Grimsby into the final. Grimsby takes it in a man-on-man against Slider Vickery.

But even Grimsby's win, with a slick 38 points, doesn't faze me. I feel like a senseless robot. I try to act excited, but Grimsby himself seems less than thrilled when he's handed the top prize: a trophy, plus a new board.

Grimsby and I and all of Whaler's Cove are losing Surfer Dog.

After the contest McCoy and I sit on the beach with a couple of Gatorades. Our dog lies between us, looking up at one, then the other, as we try to piece together how Mackie—a nickname for McCoy—showed up in Whaler's Cove.

It seems that McCoy had been at a regional surf contest on this same beach. Afterward he had settled the dog in the backseat of his van and headed home to Santa Barbara. He met a friend for dinner in Crystal Bay. It was a warm evening; McCoy slid back the van's sunroof and left Mackie asleep on his blanket. "When I got back, Mackie was gone."

After calling the police, McCoy searched until midnight, then checked into a motel. He combed the town all the following day; no one remembered seeing the dog.

"I ran an ad in the *Harbor Times* for the next month, but got no answers. I figured Mackie had been stolen. Maybe he was, and somehow got away."

"He wouldn't have left the van on his own," I say.

"Except for one reason." McCoy grins. "To chase after a female dog.

"Whatever the reason he got out," McCoy goes on, "once Mackie realized I was gone, he probably headed back to the place where we were last together. The beach here at Whaler's Cove."

"A whole thirty miles?"

"I've heard of dogs finding their masters several states away."

"Blackie's that kind of dog."

"Mackie," McCoy corrects.

At the sound of the name, dark bulging eyes turn to McCoy.

"So how did you teach him to surf?" I ask.

McCoy laughs. "I'm pretty sure Mackie taught *me*!"

"But you trained him to do the other stuff, right? I've never seen such a good dog."

"Wasn't my doing. Huh, boy?" He reaches over and chucks the dog's chin. Just that little gesture makes me jealous. "Mackie was raised by the family next door to me. The Murphys. He was supposed to be a guide dog for the blind. That's the reason he minds so well. Those dogs have to be perfect."

"So that's why he stops at corners and waits for traffic."

"Yep. And all the rest. Never jumps up. Never begs. Never climbs on furniture. Well, you know."

McCoy goes on with his story. "When Mackie was eighteen months old, he was sent to the Guide Dog Center for his final training. But he washed out. So the Murphys kept him. Great family. When they moved to Santa Fe, they gave him to me. Couldn't think of taking Mackie away from the surf."

"But how come Blackie washed out? He's . . . he *is* perfect!"

McCoy pats the dog again. "*I* sure think so. But the trainers said he had an 'obsession.' That's something that distracts the dog from his job. It could be anything. Cars. Other animals. Or food. Just a moment's lapse, for a blind person, could mean disaster."

"And Blackie?"

"Can't you guess?" He points to a perfect wave, peaking, then rolling smoothly toward shore. "Mackie's obsessed with water."

Obsessed. There's that word again.

McCoy drives me home and helps me break the news to Mom. Or is it me helping him?

When I introduce McCoy, he seems really embarrassed. He hunches his big shoulders, and he won't look at Mom, keeps his eyes on Blackie. "Uh, ma'am. Your dog . . ."

"Yes?"

"Your dog is *my* dog," he blurts. "I mean, you see, Blackie belongs to me."

Mom takes it pretty well. "I see." She turns pale, but keeps her voice steady. "Why, yes. You mean, this is Mackie?"

"Yes, ma'am."

"Mackie. Lost Mackie." Her words sound as if she's reading them. "Of course. We're so happy you've found your dog." She looks McCoy over, from his sunglasses to his sandals, as if sizing him up. You can almost see what she's thinking: Is this someone's idea of a joke? Is this McCoy telling the truth? And, even so, is he a good enough human being to deserve a dog like Blackie?

She makes a weak stab at hospitality. "Can I give you a Coke, some iced tea?"

"Thanks, ma'am, I have to run."

"All right. I guess I'd better . . . get his things together."

Blackie, tail wagging, follows her from room to room as she packs his mattress, blanket, and toys. She hands over the dog's medical records and ties up his bag of kibble. She takes several plastic containers of kidney and livers from the freezer and puts them into a sack. "He's especially fond of the kidney."

Matt McCoy says to Mom, "Mackie was lucky to find such a good home."

"*We* were the lucky ones." She looks away and dabs at her eyes with the sleeve of her sweatshirt. My nose is all runny from holding back the tears. I can't wait to be alone in my room.

I bring the old dog collar downstairs and show the tag to McCoy. MACKIE.

"I called this number, but you'd moved."

McCoy says, "I'm really glad you tried."

McCoy opens the door of his van, and the dog hops onto the front seat as if he owns it. "We'll be around. I travel the coast a lot. We can stop by and visit."

Mom says, "That would be nice."

Is she crazy? I turn to McCoy. "I kind of wish you wouldn't."

"Sure. Whatever you say."

Blackie sits in the front seat of the van, panting, looking smiley, his eyes straight ahead. Doesn't he know what's happening? Doesn't he care?

McCoy gets into the van and starts the engine.

I say, "Good-bye, Blackie." In answer, he turns to me with, "Woof." That's it. One measly "Woof." Then he looks back at McCoy.

We watch the two drive away. I feel like my heart will burst and splatter all over the sidewalk. I rush into the house, dash to my room, and lock the door.

At dinner that night no one says a word except "Please pass the butter." Finally, Dad says, "We can get another dog."

"No dog," I say. "I don't want another dog. Not ever again."

"I'm with you," says Mom. "Another dog would be— just another dog."

13 Going It Alone

I stand at the kitchen work center, helping Mom make oatmeal cookies. It's a dumb way to spend the afternoon, but I'm not up for much else.

"Put a teaspoon of dough on the cookie sheet," she says, "then flatten it with the bottom of the glass dipped in sugar."

Dip, squash. Dip, squash. Every now and then I sneak a bite of the raw dough.

"So what's with the surfing?" says Mom. "You haven't been in days."

"Dunno. Just don't feel like it."

"Without your dog, you mean."

"That's part of it, I guess." Dip, squash. "I'm kind of taking a vacation from the board. Sort of sick of it."

"I don't believe what I'm hearing."

"Spring winds. Small waves. Not much fun."

Mom gives me one of her X-ray looks. "Poor surf never stopped you before."

"Thought I might hang around for after-school sports. Hit a few baseballs."

"You don't sound very excited about it."

"I'm not."

"Then why do it?"

"Thought you wanted me to make friends."

She puts the cookie sheet in the oven and sets the timer. "You miss him terribly, don't you?"

In the two weeks since Blackie left, by some kind of silent agreement, no one has spoken his name. "Don't *you* miss him, Mom?"

"Of course." She puts her hands on my shoulders. Her apron is all floury. "Pete, I'm worried about you. You have to snap out of this funk."

Sure, just like that, put on a ten-tooth smile.

"I told you. You were too dependent on that dog."

"You don't understand, Mom. Nothing's fun anymore."

She couldn't possibly understand. No matter where I go, Blackie's shadow follows. A big black shadow that hides the sun and turns the whole world gray. "Not even surfing's the same. I feel like such a loser."

"You do very well for your age. Didn't Grimsby say so?"

"Yeah, I'm amazing. First heat, an eight-year-old makes me look like a complete idiot."

Mom nods. "So *that's* it." She puts away the sugar and

sets the spices back into their alphabetical places on the shelf. The kitchen begins to smell of cinnamon.

"What's that business you always give me? 'Surfers compete only against themselves.' 'Every good ride is a win'?" She rinses the mixing bowl and clangs it into the draining rack. "So why do you care what some kid does?"

"I got to thinking I was pretty hot. But without Blackie I can't do squat. *He* was the surfer. I just tagged along."

"That's not so, Pete. Stop beating yourself up."

"It's true. I'm a loser. I'm a phony. I just don't have it. Without Blackie I'm like a crummy beginner."

"So you're going to give up surfing?"

I slump into the kitchen chair. "Nope."

And right then I realize something. Surfing is what I do. And no matter how it kills me to surf without Blackie, I have to keep trying. Once you're a surfer, a real surfer, it's like you don't even have a choice. I turn to Mom. "Nope. Can't do that either."

"I didn't think so."

The timer bell rings; she takes the cookies from the oven. "So what *are* you going to do?"

"Dunno."

"I'd say you'd better get out and practice."

"First you ground me so I can't surf; now you nag me to practice. I wish you guys would make up your minds."

"We are not *guys*," she says, but she's smiling. "Why don't you take some cookies to your surfer friends?"

. . .

I go upstairs to put on the tight wet suit. No Blackie. No talent. No friends. Talk about a zero life.

But I'm trying, anyway. I tell myself making friends is like another contest. Maybe things at school will get better if I practice. I've asked myself, Why did everyone like my dog? Probably because he was so friendly, loved everyone. When he panted, he looked like he was smiling. So I try to smile, even when I don't feel like it. Now sometimes even girls smile back and say, "Hi." At least I'm not invisible anymore.

Downstairs I grab the bag of cookies and take my board from the laundry room. At the door I stop and turn around.

In the kitchen I pick up the phone and tell Mom, "Maybe I'll give old Brill a call."

Actually, Brill isn't half bad. In fact, he's pretty amazing. Completely fearless, like Blackie. He's clumsy and off balance and eats it a lot, but as soon as he pops up, he climbs on the board and shoots seaward, ready to get nailed again. Lucky the spring waves are small; otherwise, the guy'd be in the hospital.

Every day, unless the surf is totally blown out, Brill and I work the wind swell in front of his house. He's a pretty good guy, in spite of his name label clothes and his flip phone. Come to think of it, I like him a lot.

On weekends, when I meet up with Grimsby and the

better surfers, Brill watches from a respectful distance and takes in every move.

Grimsby and I are still friendly, but he's pretty much given up on me, as far as coaching. I never should have told him I didn't want to compete. He probably thinks I'm a poor loser. I probably am.

So now I'm left to figure things out myself. Each time I head out to sea, I try to picture Blackie leading the way. Which wave would he take? Turn or wait? Sometimes I guess right; just as often I miss. With every good wave, right after I kick out, I still find myself searching the shore for Blackie, listening for his bark of approval.

At night I still wad up a couple of pillows to make a lump at the foot of my bed. I pretend Blackie's lying on my feet. It's the only way I can get to sleep.

Is there any cure for loving a dog?

14 June Gloom

June creeps in, as usual, in a cloud of gloom, with mists over the shoreline and the lonely sound of foghorns. The end of school is the only bright spot. On second thought, not exactly.

It's the end of school for most people, but not for me. My math turned mediocre, history downright disastrous. So after a week off, I'll be shuffling back to summer school. I can surf afternoons and weekends, but only after I've finished a ton of schoolwork.

Along with the grim news about summer school came a "little talk," of course. Something like this.

"You remember telling me," says Mom, "about how Blackie failed in his guide dog training?"

"Because he loved the water too much."

"I believe the word was 'obsessed'?"

"So?"

"His obsession prevented him from achieving what he was meant to do."

"Blackie was meant to be a surfer dog," I say.

But I get her point.

On the last day of school we get out early. I meet Brill at his house for lunch. Although it's kind of damp, we eat our BLTs on the patio so we can watch the surfers. The beach has its first crowd of summer vacationers, little kids with sand pails, pests with Frisbees, moms with ice chests.

Along with our smoothies, Brill brings out a couple of entry blanks for another WSA contest, a week from Saturday. "We're going to enter, right?"

"Hadn't really thought about it."

Not true. I'd thought about it a lot, and I wanted to enter, sort of. I mean I really wanted to enter, but I didn't want my butt kicked by an eight-year-old.

"Come on. It'll be laughs. Good experience."

I could use some of Brill's just-for-fun attitude. But being casual isn't easy when you know you have a fair chance of winning. And I just might.

I've been running wind sprints lately and paddle-racing around the buoy. Darned hard work, but it seems to be paying off. The turns are coming easier, and Grimsby seems to think I'm surfing more aggressively.

Brill hands me the blank; it has a grease spot from mayonnaise. "Let's go for it, Pete. What do we have to lose?"

"Yeah, right," I try to convince myself. "So we end up in the cellar. Who cares?"

But I do care. After all my workouts, I *could* end up in the cellar. That's what they call "experience," and I want no part of it.

Besides the whiz kid Patches, I'll have another problem. This being WSA, Matt McCoy will probably show—with Blackie. And meeting up with the dog could ruin everything.

After lunch we turn in our blanks at the surf shop. Grimsby's working that afternoon. He looks at me kind of funny, one eyebrow raised. "So you're ready to charge again?"

I say I guess so.

Then he turns to Brill. "This your first?"

"Yeah," says Brill, "but I'm just along for the ride."

"Only way to go," says Grimsby.

I get his message.

The morning of the regionals comes up bright and sunny, cooled by gusty winds from the northwest. Next to the Blackbeard judges' tent they've put up a grandstand, with reserved seats selling for $6 each. Mom and Dad have two tickets but aren't going to show until the twelve and under begin.

I cross the dunes toward the judges' tent, and, sure enough, there they are: McCoy and Blackie. To avoid them, I cut a diagonal across the beach and head north toward Mouse Rock.

McCoy spots me. "Hey, Pete. Wait up."

I wave but keep on walking. I can feel the shakes coming on.

McCoy breaks into a run and catches up, Blackie beside him. "Hey, what's with you, dude? You mad or something?"

"Sorry, it's just that I . . ."

Blackie greets me with barks and licks, same as always. I can't resist kneeling and wrapping my arms around his happy wiggles. He's put on weight. How could anyone have fed him better than Mom did?

"Still feels like he's yours, huh?" says McCoy.

I let go and straighten up. "Not at all."

But that *is* the way I feel. As if McCoy has stolen him. It's crazy to be angry. But I can't help myself.

"I could use a favor," says McCoy.

Sure. Take my dog, wreck my life, then ask a favor.

"I have a new job," he says. "With Blackbeard."

"Congratulations." I'm watching the dog and don't look up.

"I'm going to be traveling a lot of the time."

"That's nice." What does the guy want? A pat on the back?

"I hate the thought of leaving Mackie in a kennel. So I was hoping you'd let him come visit now and then."

Dog-sit? The guy can't be serious. "Don't think so."

McCoy looks surprised. "No chance?"

"Couldn't handle it."

McCoy nods. "Okay. I get you."

We walk along the wet sand, not talking, making tracks side by side. Finally McCoy says, "Sorry. I guess I was only thinking of Mackie. What a great time he'd have."

Blackie nudges me with his nose; I ignore him. I pick up a shell, spin it across the water. "Look, it was hard enough to let him go the first time."

"I said I was sorry," says McCoy.

The P.A. system calls the boys' division contestants to check in.

"Gotta go." I turn and race down the beach, an earthquake rattling my bones.

15 What's to Lose?

We straddle our boards, waiting for the blast of the air horn. Brill is to my right, and to my left is Patches Pauley.

I paddle out toward my first wave. The swells are large and strong, but the wind and whitecaps are turning them to mush. It's hard to judge the peaks.

When the horn sounds, I paddle for all I'm worth. I catch the first wave, snap it off the top, and ease a backside floater through the heavy whitewater. I can feel my knees quaking, try to focus on Grimsby's words. "Relax, man. Let go. Enjoy!" Sure thing. Who could enjoy this blown out mess?

The second wave is not much better. I drop in, dig a rail off the bottom, correct my footing, then manage a small aerial. Not bad, but nothing spectacular. The third wave I misjudge completely and go over the falls. Shoot. From here on in I'll really have to put it together. But my legs feel like rubber, and I'm already tired from paddling against the wind.

Here comes Brill. He's caught a monster. His takeoff is shaky, but he survives the drop and gets a good, long ride, with a couple of clean turns just ahead of the curl.

Now comes Pauley on my left, stroking out to grab the wave I'm heading for. But he's got position on me and takes off, shredding. First a frontside rail grab through a folding section. Then, after a couple of speed turns, ends with a nice snapback. A style like no other—he'll be tough to beat.

I can see Grimsby waving from the beach, motioning me to move seaward. But farther out, the choppy water makes it hard to spot the large swells.

I sit on my board, waiting for a new set. Only seven minutes to go, and, except for whitecaps, the sea looks flat. In the distance I spot a swell. Yes, bigger, bigger. But Patches spots it, too, and starts moving. Patches will have the right of way, unless I can catch a swell farther out. I take the chance, meet it early, then paddle like crazy and hope it will carry me.

One, two, here we go! But the wave slides from under me. Patches, about twenty-five feet nearer the shore, whips his board around for a late takeoff, sticks the bottom turn. The next thing I see is a series of sprays as he destroys the lip all the way down the line.

The swells that follow would have given fair rides, but now I'm too far out. I can float and wait or, since time is running out, paddle in to take the smaller waves. In or out, in or out? Make up your mind, chicken.

Brill paddles out to meet me. "Hey, it's pumpin'." He keeps going, looking for the big one. No sweat, he's only here for laughs.

A new set is nowhere in sight. I have too much time to think, to tie myself in knots. My stomach feels like it's full of wet sand, my heart's a tom-tom, my muscles tighter than the wet suit.

I can see Brill's blue-and-gold-striped suit bobbing out beyond me. He's lying on his board like he's about to take a nap.

The wind blows stronger. Whitecaps lap against my board, splash my eyes with salt spray. Five minutes to go and still no swells. This is what they call fun?

I'm sitting there, teed off about the whole competition thing, when, like a wave in the face, it hits me. What if Brill, who couldn't care less, gets the big one and shows me up?

I can almost see him, zooming into shore, getting super-fancy on some giant crest he's caught by dumb luck. So the honyaking amateur beats me out of the heat, showing off all the stuff I taught him. Thanks a lot, friend.

No way, Brill. I'm coming after you.

With long, deep strokes I paddle seaward. Might as well gamble on one great honking ride. And if I blow it? Well, as Grimsby says . . .

As I head out, I look again toward the beach, just in

time to see Blackie, leash dangling, dash into the water. McCoy whistles to him, then shouts, but the dog keeps on paddling into the rough surf.

Now he's beyond the breakline and swimming straight toward me.

"Hey, boy!"

Blackie catches up with me, and we both swim at a fast clip toward the horizon.

And there it is, the wave of the day, rising right above us. I scratch up its face to the top and pull my board around for a one-paddle takeoff. I pull with all my strength and jump to my feet. My heart's screaming as I see the wall ledging in front of me. But I stay cool, stall a little on the tail, and drag my hand on the face as I pull into a backdoor barrel!

I don't know how long I'm in there or how far I'm traveling. All I know is that I finally shoot out of the tube onto the shoulder in a jet spray of salt water. I can hear the crowd shouting and Grimsby yelling, "You killed it!"

The emcee, who happens to be McCoy, shakes my hand and holds up the boys' division trophy. The crowd applauds. Blackie barks.

"And Blackbeard's gift for the winner is their new Predator Megastretch 2002 wet suit." He unfolds a titanium zipperless suit with a comet streaking across the chest.

I feel like a film star. I watch my folks' proud faces as I

take the microphone. Mom's snapping pictures like mad, and Dad's peering through the camcorder.

"Thanks a lot, everyone." I lean down and pat Blackie's head. "And I'd like to thank my fellow surfer for his support."

The crowd cheers and whistles. "Yea, Surfer Dog."

But I know I won the day on my own. After the first heat, McCoy hustled Blackie off the beach and locked him inside his van. And I was so busy shredding two heats against Patches, I didn't notice the dog was gone.

16 Hang Loose, Champ

After my folks leave, I hang around to help clean up. I'm not quite ready to end this day.

Because Blackbeard is a sponsor and McCoy a judge, he didn't enter the contest. Which allowed Grimsby once again to take first in the men's. Now the two of them are dismantling the judges' tent. "Nice work," says McCoy. "Hang around your phone. You'll probably get lots of offers."

"Now that *you're* leaving the coast," says Grimsby with his one-sided grin. He takes the pieces of metal frame and heads for McCoy's van.

Brill comes by, wearing a Blackbeard T-shirt, prize for the consolation heat. McCoy waves to him. "Good going. You're on you're way."

"Thanks," says Brill. "I learned a lot." He turns to me. "We're going to Monterey tomorrow. Grandma's birth-day." He picks up his board. "So I'll see you Monday."

"Not till afternoon," I say. "I'll be in summer school, remember?"

"Me, too. I signed up for that advanced computer stuff." He waves an overall "See ya" and heads for his house.

"You guys are smart," says McCoy. "No one ever gets shafted for knowing too much."

I tell him, "That's what I figure."

I fold the leftover T-shirts and posters and gather up the leftover ham-and-cheese sandwiches. "Don't put them in the van just yet," calls McCoy. "Mackie's probably hungry."

I put down the carton and feel the bottom drop out of my gut. In the excitement of the contest, I'd almost forgotten. Blackie's not mine anymore.

McCoy makes several trips to his van with the rolled-up judge's tent and the P.A. system. He says, "Want a ride home?"

"Thanks. I have my bike."

Through his teeth McCoy whistles "Barrel Blues" while we pile in the rest of the boxes. Blackie's resting in the back of the van—on the bed he used in my room, next to the water bowl Mom bought him. I notice the sunroof is open only partway. McCoy's not taking the chance of losing his dog again. When I shove in the carton of sandwiches, Blackie immediately becomes alert, sniffs the box, but doesn't beg. McCoy rewards him with a half.

McCoy climbs in the van and starts the engine. "See ya next time," he says. "Hang loose, champ."

The van roars off, and Blackie, nosing the sandwich carton, doesn't even look up.

17 It's Over

I ride my bike down Ocean Boulevard, watching the fog roll in, first in small puffs, then a great cloud that covers what would have been a perfect sunset.

My dog didn't even look up when he left. I feel more mad than sad. I may never see Blackie again. Even worse, I might. He may keep showing up at contests, each time shredding my insides.

During the contest, when Blackie dashed into the waves, I thought he'd come back—that he'd made a choice between me and McCoy. It seemed like he was with me, even when McCoy locked him in the van. That's probably what kept me going through the next two heats, why I was able to outmaneuver Patches Pauley. I was Blackie's real master, his hero.

But I was wrong. Twice now Blackie's driven away in that van, without so much as a turn in my direction. When he's mine, he's happy. When McCoy takes him back, he's still happy. Blackie goes with the flow. Whatever happens, happens; it's okay by him. Whoever holds the ham sandwich wins.

I skid my bike to a stop in front of the surf shop, take another look at the Channel Islands tri-fin in the window. If I save my allowance, do some yard work, maybe get a paper route, by the time the fall contest rolls around I might be able to buy it. Now that I'm a prizewinner, I have a reputation to hang on to. Like Blackie, I'm getting on with my life. Whatever happens, happens.

Back on my bike I turn left on Birch Street and begin the tough climb up our hill. I try to do it without shifting; it's good for the wind. Halfway up the block, a scroungy little dog dashes off someone's porch, yapping for all he's worth. He jumps at my bike, yip, yip, acting like his mini-teeth could tear my leg off. Just then a car comes around the corner and barely misses him. Brakes squeal, then the car roars on up the hill.

"Hey, mutt! Watch it!" My bike tips over, and there I am in the middle of Birch Street with that idiotic pup licking my face. I get up, roll my bike to the curb, and grab the dog.

An old lady in an apron is standing on the porch calling, "Caesar, you naughty thing."

I trudge across the lawn and hand the lady her mutt, which couldn't weigh more than five pounds. Who does he think he is, attacking bicycles?

The lady thanks me and apologizes. "Just got him today. Didn't know he was a chaser."

I walk my bike the rest of the hill, and I keep thinking about that warm, wiggly mutt, almost too little to live. And I think about the dog pound, full of funny-looking half-breeds, yapping, standing on hind legs, begging people to save them from death row.

I come home to a celebration dinner. I can smell the smoke from Dad's barbecued T-bones; Mom's fixed her special cheesy baked potatoes. "And save room for raspberry chocolate cake," she says as she heaps my plate.

We talk about the contest, and Mom says things like, "Weren't you scared when the waves got so high?" Dad tells me, "Surfing must take a lot of coordination. Like skiing."

And I say, "Like skiing. Only with the ground moving under you."

I finish my steak and realize I've left a little meat on the bone, like I used to for Blackie.

Never mind, I'm getting on with my life. I gnaw the last gristly bite and think again about the shaggy little mutt. The bone clanks on my plate. Nope, no other dog. It wouldn't be fair. I'd always be comparing him to my surfer dog. Blackie can forget about me, but he's stuck in my head forever.

The doorbell rings. "I'll get it," says Dad. "Probably the paperboy collecting."

But it's not the paperboy. It's Matt McCoy. And he's not smiling.

18 Out of the Fog

You want a dog?" McCoy says in a loud voice, to no one in particular.

"Come in," says Dad, polite but puzzled.

Through the open door I can hear Blackie whining and barking in the van.

McCoy stays on the porch. "Take him." He sounds almost angry. "He's all yours."

Mom and I join Dad in the entry hall. "I don't get you," I say.

"You hear that racket?" McCoy nods toward the van, which is almost hidden by the fog. "That's been going on for the last couple of hours. Nearly drove me off the road."

With giant steps McCoy leaves the porch, stomps to the van, opens it. Blackie races up the walk, squealing. I kneel and catch him in my arms. He's impossible to hold, races to Mom, then starts galloping around the living room. McCoy shrugs and repeats, "He's *yours*."

I whistle at Blackie and order him to sit. He skids on the hardwood floor, comes to a stop, and sits, panting and smiling. His eyes are on his master. Me.

"Should have known," said McCoy. "First he breaks loose on the beach and dashes into the water. Then, when I lock him in the van, he barks his brains out."

"He did? During the contest? When we loaded, he was snoozing."

"That's because I'd let him out to see you," says McCoy. "When I gave you your prize, and everyone cheered, Blackie felt he was home again."

Blackie. He called his dog *Blackie*.

"It wasn't until I drove off that Blackie realized you weren't with us. He let out the most god-awful howl. And he wouldn't shut up."

Blackie sits quietly, glancing back and forth between us. "But . . . but I can't take your dog," I say, not meaning a word of it.

McCoy shoves his hands into his pockets. "Like I have a choice?"

Everyone's quiet now, the clock tick-tocks in the hall; the fireplace crackles; we hear foghorns in the distance.

"See how fat Blackie's getting?" says McCoy. "Hardly ever gets to swim."

True, the dog is a little lumpy in spots.

"Blackie knows where he wants to be. On the beach." He smiles, but just barely. "With an up-and-coming surfer."

Mom snaps her fingers; Blackie goes to her. She strokes his ears.

"And with a mom," says McCoy, "who feeds him kidney and livers."

"If you're sure that's what you want," Mom says a little too quickly. "We'll take good care of him."

Mom looks up at McCoy, who's blinking his eyes and turning toward the door. She gets to her feet and with her cheeriest voice says, "We have an extra steak. Why don't you stay for dinner?"

"Better not," says McCoy. "It'll be a long, slow trip to Santa Barbara." He opens the front door to the fog. His voice gets foggy, too. "But I know what you can do with the steak."

That all happened a few years back, but I can still see the look on McCoy's face as he stepped into the cold dark mist. We never saw him again; I hear he's settled in Australia, where Blackbeard has its headquarters.

I fasten the tri-fin on the surf racks of my Volkswagen and load my bags into the trunk. Blackie's watching my every move. He seems a little on edge, senses something's up. I know he'll miss me, but Mom has promised to give him a beach run every day. And to take a towel along.

After lunch I'm heading for my dorm at U.C. Santa Barbara. I had my choice of any U. of California school.

When people ask, "Why not Berkeley?" I say, "Ever surfed Rincon Point at sunset?"

I'll probably study law, like Dad. But I know one thing for sure. I won't be a lawyer who surfs.

I'll be a surfer who practices law.

Pete's Surfer-Speak

aerial fakey: An aerial maneuver in which the surfer grabs the rail of the board in midair and spins 180 degrees, landing backward with the tail of the board in front of him.

boneyard: The whitewater area between the breaking wave and the beach; sometimes a rocky shallow area to be avoided.

goofy foot: Most surfers ride with the left foot forward. A goofy foot leads with the right foot.

grommet: A young inexperienced surfer.

honyaker: A clumsy surfer, an amateur, a kook, a beginner.

sponger: One who rides a foam boogie board, on his belly.

stick: To make a perfect landing, also slang for surfboard.

tri-fin: A surfboard with three fins, currently the most popular design.